SOPHIE'S TOM

"An enchanting tale... Dick King-Smith has done it again." *Child Education*

Dick King-Smith used to be a farmer and is now one of the world's favourite children's book authors. Winner of the Guardian Fiction Award for *The Sheep-Pig* (filmed as *Babe*), he was named Children's Book Author of the Year in 1991 and won the 1995 Children's Book Award for *Harriet's Hare*. His titles for Walker include the Read and Wonder non-fiction picture books *All Pigs Are Beautiful* and *I Love Guinea-Pigs*, as well as *Puppy Love, Dick King-Smith's Animal Friends* and *The Finger Eater*.

David Parkins has illustrated a number of children's books, including the picture books *No Problem, Prowlpuss* (shortlisted for the 1994 Kurt Maschler Award and the Smarties Book Prize), *Aunt Nancy and Old Man Trouble* and *Aunt Nancy and Cousin Lazybones*.

D0589530

Sophie, though small,
was very determined.

SOPHIE'S TOM

Written by
DICK KING-SMITH

Illustrated by
DAVID PARKINS

TED SMART

First published 1991 by
Walker Books Ltd, 87 Vauxhall Walk
London SE11 5HJ

This edition published 2001 for
The Book People Ltd, Hall Wood Avenue
Haydock, St Helens WA11 9UL

2 4 6 8 10 9 7 5 3 1

This book has been typeset in Plantin.

Printed and bound in Great Britain by
The Guernsey Press Co. Ltd

British Library Cataloguing in Publication Data
A catalogue record for this book is
available from the British Library.

ISBN 0-7445-7726-8

CONTENTS

*Sophie woke early on the morning
of her fifth birthday.*

IN WHICH TOM APPEARS

Sophie woke early on the morning of her fifth birthday. It was still very dark. Usually the first thing she did when she had switched on the light was to look at the pictures hanging on her bedroom walls. There were four of them, all drawn by Sophie's mother who was clever at that sort of thing.

One was of a cow called Blossom, one was of two hens named April and May, the third of a Shetland pony called Shorty and the fourth of a spotty pig by the name of Measles.

These were the animals that would one day in the future belong to Sophie, for she was, she said, going to be a lady farmer when she grew up; and neither Sophie's mother and father nor her seven-year-old twin brothers, Matthew and Mark, doubted for one moment that she would.

Sophie, though small, was very determined.

But on this particular morning Sophie did not spare a glance for her portrait gallery. Instead she scrambled to the end of her bed and peered over. And there it was!

"Yikes!" cried Sophie. "He's been!" and she undid the safety-pin that fastened the long bulging woollen stocking to the bedclothes.

By now Sophie was used to the fact that her birthday was on Christmas Day. The twins, who had been born in spring, felt rather sorry for her.

"Poor old Sophie," said Matthew, "being born then."

"Hard luck on her," said Mark. "Glad we weren't."

But Sophie didn't mind.

"It's twice as nice," she said, when anyone asked how she felt about it. "Everybody gives me two presents."

"It was clever of you, Mum," she had said to her mother once.

"What was?"

"Having me on Christmas Day. How did you manage it?"

"With difficulty. But you were the nicest possible Christmas present. Daddy and I both wanted a little girl very much."

"Why?"

"Well, we already had two boys, didn't we?"

"What would you have called me if I'd been a boy?"

"Noël, probably."

"Yuk!" said Sophie. "I'm glad I wasn't, then."

This Christmas Day, the sixth of Sophie's life, started off in the customary way. As soon as the grandmother clock in the hall had struck seven, the twins ran, and Sophie plodded, into their parents' bedroom, and they all climbed on to the big bed to show what Father Christmas had brought them.

Then, after breakfast, came the ceremony of the present-giving.

This was always done in the same way. Everybody sat down, in the sitting-room of course – at least the two grown-ups sat down with their cups of coffee, while Matthew and Mark danced about with

*Matthew and Mark danced about, and Sophie
stood stolidly beside the Christmas tree.*

excitement, and their sister stood stolidly beside the Christmas tree, beneath which all the presents were arranged, and waited for the others to sing "Happy birthday, dear Sophie, happy birthday to you!"

Then the opening of the presents began, one at a time, youngest first, eldest last – a Christmas present for Sophie, then one for Mark, then Matthew (ten minutes older), then Mummy, then Dad, and finally a birthday present for Sophie, before she began again on her next Christmas one.

This year, to Sophie's surprise and delight, word of her intention to be a lady farmer had somehow got round the entire family, and both her Christmas and her birthday presents reflected this.

From grandparents and aunts and uncles came picture books of farms and story books of farms and colouring books of farms. Best of all, from her mother and father, there was (for Christmas) a model farmyard with a cowshed and a barn and some post-and-rail fences and a duck pond made of a piece of glass in one corner and (for her birthday) lots of little model animals, cows and sheep and horses, some standing up, some lying down, and a fierce-looking bull, chickens, a turkey-cock, some ducks for the pond, and even a spotty pig.

And as for her present from the twins – that was super, nothing less than a red tractor pulling a yellow trailer!

"The tractor's for your birthday," said Matthew.

"And the trailer's for Christmas," said Mark.

"What a lovely present!" said Sophie's mother.

"Yes," said the twins with one voice.
"It was jolly expensive too."

"Yes," said the twins with one voice. "It was jolly expensive too."

Sophie felt a bit guilty about this, since her Christmas present to them was the usual one – a Mars bar each, their favourite. Still, that was all she could manage when she had finished buying presents for her parents. Afterwards she had unscrewed the plug in the tummy of her piggy-bank, on whose side was stuck a notice:

FARM MUNNY
THANK YOU
SOPHIE

and found that there was only seven pence of her savings left.

At last there was only one present remaining at the foot of the tree, an ordinary white envelope with SOPHIE written on it.

Underneath there was some joined-up writing that Sophie couldn't read. She had left it till last because it looked boring. Probably just an old Christmas card, she thought, as she picked it up and handed it to her father.

"What's it say, Daddy?" she asked.

"It says:

SOPHIE

Many happy returns of Christmas Day
Love from Aunt Al."

Aunt Al was Sophie's Great-great-aunt Alice, who was nearly eighty-one years old and lived in the Highlands of Scotland. She had come to lunch one day in the summer, and she and Sophie had got on like a house on fire.

"Aren't you going to open it?" asked Sophie's mother.

"It's just a card, I expect," said Sophie, but inside the envelope was another smaller envelope marked FARM MONEY and inside that was a five pound note.

"Yikes!" shouted Sophie. "I could buy a hen with that, a real one, I mean!"

"April," said Mark.

"Or May," said Matthew.

"You wait till you get your real farm," said Sophie's father. "This house would be full of animals if you had your way."

After lunch, Sophie set out her model farm on the sitting-room floor. She loaded all the animals in turn on to the trailer, and then drove the tractor into the yard to unload and arrange them.

"You're lucky," she said, holding up the turkey-cock. "We've just been eating one of your lot. Mind you, when I have real turkeys on my farm, I shan't eat any of them."

"You going to be a vegetarian?" asked her mother.

"No," said Sophie, "but you can't eat your friends. I shall eat a stranger – from the supermarket."

"This farm of yours is just going to be a collection of pets," said her father, yawning in his armchair.

"That's right," said Sophie. "I like pets. I wish I had a pet, now."

"You're much too young."

"I'm five."

"That's much too young," said the twins.

"I'll buy myself a pet, with Aunt Al's money."

"Don't be silly," said her father sleepily.

"I'm not silly."

"You are," said Matthew.

"I'm not."

*"You can't eat your friends," said Sophie.
"I shall eat a stranger from the supermarket."*

"You are," said Mark.

"I AM NOT."

"Be quiet, Sophie," said her mother, "and play with your toy farm. Daddy wants a nap."

Sophie put the turkey-cock down (on the duck pond, as it happened) and stamped out of the room. Hands rammed deep into the pockets of her jeans, she plodded out into the wintry garden, a short stocky figure whose dark hair looked, as always, as though she had just come through a hedge backwards. Her head was bent, there was a scowl on her round face, and as she walked along the path beside the garden wall, she mouthed the phrase that she always used to describe those who upset her.

"Mowldy, stupid, and assive!" she muttered. "That's what they all are, mowldy, stupid, and assive. Why can't I have a real live animal of my own – now?"

"Nee-ow?" said a voice above her head, and, looking up, Sophie saw a cat sitting on the wall. It was a jet-black cat with huge round orange eyes that stared down at her, and again it said, more confidently, "Nee-ow!"

Then it jumped down, trotted up to her with its tail held stiffly upright, and began to rub itself against her legs, purring like a steam-engine.

Sophie's frown gave way to a huge grin as she stroked the gleaming sable fur. "Happy Christmas, my dear!" she said. "And how beautiful you are! I wonder who you belong to?"

"Yee-ew!" said the cat.

At least that's how it sounded to Sophie.

"You come along with me, my dear," said Sophie,
"and we'll see what we can find."

IN WHICH TOM
DISAPPEARS

Sophie's first thought was to fetch the cat something to eat. All animals must be regularly fed, she knew, and this one was sure to be hungry even though it looked so sleek and healthy. Anyway it was Christmas Day, when everybody eats more than they should.

"So you come along with me, my dear," said Sophie, "and we'll see what we can find."

She glanced at the sitting-room window, but no one was looking out. They were all used to Sophie's tantrums, which did not really last long and were best left to blow themselves over. So she plodded round to the back of the house and in through the door that led to the kitchen. The cat followed close at heel, just as though it had been following Sophie all its life and just as though it knew what would happen next. It watched as Sophie opened the door of the fridge, and pulled some bits of skin from the remains of the turkey. She put them on a saucer, with half a leftover chipolata and some bits of bacon rind that her mother had put aside for the bird-table.

"Help yourself," she said to the black cat. "Whatever-your-name-is." She watched it eating.

"Actually," she said, "you'd better have a name, hadn't you? Trouble is, I don't know if you're a boy or a girl, and you can't tell me, can you?"

"Nee-o," said the cat, raising its head from the empty saucer.

"I think you're a boy," said Sophie, "because you're greedy. So I shall call you Tom." She took a milk bottle from the fridge and poured some into the saucer and some into a glass.

"Cheers, Tom!" said Sophie, and they both drank.

Her mother came into the kitchen.

"Sophie!" she said. "What on earth are you doing?"

"I'm giving my cat a drink of milk," said Sophie, reasonably.

"Your cat?"

"He says he's mine," said Sophie.

"Oh don't be silly. It probably belongs to the people next door. No, come to think of it, they don't have a cat. It must be a stray."

"What's a stray?"

"A cat or a dog that's lost or hasn't got a home."

"Well, this one can't be a stray, Mummy," said Sophie, "because he's got a home."

"Where?"

"Here."

"Oh no he hasn't, my girl," said Sophie's mother firmly. "That cat goes straight out of this house, now, d'you understand? Daddy doesn't like cats, you know that. Anyway it does not belong to you, it's got a perfectly good owner somewhere, and it will make its way back to its own house."

"How can he?" said Sophie. "He's lost. You said so."

The milk finished, the black cat rubbed its purring way around Sophie's mother's ankles, and automatically she bent to stroke it.

"I'm sorry, puss," she said, "but out you must go, and that is definite."

"Black cats are lucky," said Sophie.

"Out!"

"Specially if they come to you from the right-hand side. Aunt Al told me that. And Tom did."

"Do as I say, Sophie. Take that cat outside," said Sophie's mother, bracing herself for a tantrum.

To her surprise Sophie simply said, "OK, I'll just put my wellies on and my coat – it's cold outside." When she had done so, she regarded her mother with a look of deep disapproval and added, "It's cold for cats too," and marched out, Tom following.

At the bottom of the garden was an old potting-shed, where Sophie kept her flocks and herds – of such animals, that is, as she was allowed to own.

These included woodlice, centipedes, earthworms, earwigs, slugs and snails,

The black cat hesitated on the threshold.

which lived in a variety of boxes, tins and jars. Most were allowed to come and go as they pleased, and most went, but Sophie continually replaced the losses.

Now, out of sight of the house, Sophie opened the potting-shed door and went in. The black cat hesitated on the threshold, but then, with the curiosity of all his kind, walked in. He jumped up on a large cardboard box – on the side of which was printed in black letters BAKED BEANS – sat down on the word SNALES, written in big red capitals, and proceeded to wash his face.

Sophie stood watching him. She was rubbing the tip of her nose, a sure sign of deep thought, and then she said, "I've got it! Listen, Tom, you can stay here for a bit. I'll bring you food – I bring cornflakes and biscuit crumbs and cabbage leaves for these animals anyway, so no one will notice. And you'll be quite safe – nobody comes down here in the winter – and I'll make you a nice warm bed."

First she closed the door and then she took a wooden seed tray off a shelf and lined it with an old sack. Then she lifted the black cat, with difficulty for he was quite heavy, and put him on the sack. But, with the contrariness of all his kind, he got out again, and stood by the closed door, mewing.

"I'm sorry, my dear," said Sophie firmly, "but here you must stay, and that is definite. Now out of the way, please." But, with the disdain for authority of all his kind, the cat took no notice, continuing to mew at the door.

Sophie however was more than a match for him in determination.

"Do as I say, Tom," she ordered, and when he did not move, she picked him up, plonked him down facing the wrong way, and was out of the potting-shed and had shut the door, before he could do anything about it.

At tea-time, they started by pulling the crackers and putting on paper hats. Then Sophie's father said, "What's this I hear about you bringing some stray cat into the house? Where is it now?"

Sophie disapproved of telling lies, and she had no intention of revealing the truth, so she said nothing.

"It's no good sulking," said her father.

"I am not sulking."

"She took it out into the garden," her mother said. "It will have gone by now."

"Good," said her father. "You know I don't like cats."

"What sort of cat was it?" said Matthew,

taking a huge bite of Christmas cake.

"A black one."

"Boy or girl?" said Mark, doing the same.

"Boy."

"How d'you know?" chorused the twins, with their mouths full.

"Because he bolts his food like you," said Sophie. "Boys are greedier than girls, everyone knows that."

She cut off a very small bit of cake.

"You should chew each mouthful thirty-two times," she said, and popped it in.

Like a pair of hawks, the twins watched the seemingly endless movement of her jaw, and the moment she swallowed, they shouted, "That was thirty-seven times!"

"Don't tease, boys," said their mother. "You know Sophie can only count to twenty."

Sophie was still sitting at the table when

the rest of the family had finished tea. They supposed that it was the chewing that was taking her so long. But as soon as they had left the room, Sophie bolted what was on her plate, and then took off her paper hat and quickly wrapped up some leftovers in it. Carrying this parcel of food, she let herself out of the back door and plodded off down the twilit garden.

She opened the door of the potting-shed a crack and called, "Tom! Here's your supper." But there was no mew from the dark interior.

Sophie opened the door a little wider and poked her head round. There was just enough light left to see the shapes of the boxes, tins and jars that housed her flocks and herds, and the sack-covered seed tray that was to have been Tom's bed. But there was no sign of the black cat himself.

*Sophie found a gap just wide enough
for a prisoner to escape.*

Down on hands and knees, to make sure he wasn't hiding behind something, Sophie found a gap in the boards at the back where the wood was rotten, a gap just wide enough for a prisoner to escape.

Sophie felt terribly disappointed and sad. She had been so sure, in the short time that she had known the black cat, that theirs was a special sort of friendship, yet he had deserted her.

Some children might have given way to tears, but Sophie did not approve of crying. She was determined to look on the bright side. Tom had just gone for a walk. He would come back. He would need his supper.

She found a shallow flowerpot and tipped into it the mess of cake and marzipan and icing sugar and currant bun and marmite sandwich that she had brought. She filled a biscuit tin from the old water can which she kept there for dampening her slugs with. Finally she propped the door of the potting-shed ajar. Plodding back up the garden, Sophie called, "Tom! Tom! Where are you?" but there was no answer.

Early on a wet Boxing Day morning, Sophie went down to the shed, more than half hoping to find the black cat sheltering there. But a peep round the door showed only a fat mouse sitting in the flowerpot eating Christmas cake, and throughout the rest of the holidays there was no sign of Tom.

Sophie played happily enough with her toy farm, and only her mother wondered why she was quieter than usual. No one else noticed, for Sophie's father was back at work after the break, and Matthew and Mark were, as ever, perfectly content with each other's company.

It must be the prospect of starting school, her mother decided, that was making Sophie more than usually silent and solitary, spending so much time staring out into the garden. She was worried about meeting a lot of strange children – that must be it.

"You'll like school, you know," she said.

"I know," said Sophie. "I'm looking forward to it. They'll have Farming Lessons." She still firmly believed this, even though the twins had rolled their eyes and tapped their foreheads when she mentioned it.

Her mother paused in the task of trying to make some sort of order of Sophie's dark mop of unruly hair.

"You're not worried about anything, are you, darling?" she asked.

Sophie rubbed the tip of her nose.

"Only about Tom," she said after a while.

"Who's Tom?"

"My cat. You know."

"Oh, he'll be all right. Cats are good at looking after themselves."

"I wish I could have looked after him," Sophie said.

On the morning of the last Saturday of the holidays, Sophie had just finished a game of Happy Families with her father and her brothers, who had all agreed, rather unhappily, to play with her. She was driving her cows in for milking, when her mother returned from some shopping and stood, on Sophie's right, looking down at the array of toy animals.

"School on Monday," she said.

"Yes," said Sophie. "I can do the morning milking before I go and the afternoon milking when I get back."

Her mother handed her something wrapped in a little twist of paper.

"What is it?" said Sophie.

"Just a little present. To bring you luck."

Sophie undid it.

It was a tiny model cat, a black one, with big orange eyes.

"Why," said Sophie, *"do I have to wear a skirt?"*

IN WHICH SOPHIE
GOES TO SCHOOL

Every day of the two years that the twins had been at school, Sophie had always gone too, walking down with her mother or, if the weather was horrible, going in the car. But now, for the first time, she would not walk or ride home again at a quarter to nine in the morning.

Now, at last, she was a schoolgirl.

The day had not started well.

"Why," said Sophie, "do I have to wear a skirt?"

"It's part of the school uniform," her mother said. "You can't go dressed as you like."

Sophie's usual clothes consisted of an old blue jersey with her name written on it in white letters, old jeans and, most of the time, wellies.

But this morning she stood in front of the looking-glass and saw a distinctly grumpy figure wearing a grey pleated skirt and, under a maroon cardigan, a grey shirt with a striped tie.

"These clothes are mowldy, stupid and assive!" she said.

"You look very smart," her mother said.

"You look very smart," her father said when she came down to breakfast. The twins said nothing (because they had been told to say nothing), but they looked at Sophie, and then looked at one another, and grinned. Sophie eyed their grey trousers darkly.

"It's a pity you're not Scotch boys," she said.

"Why?"

"Then you'd have to wear skirts. They do. Aunt Al told me."

When they arrived at the school, Matthew and Mark galloped off without a backward look. Sophie and her mother made their way to the reception classroom. Here they found a number of other children who were starting school for the first time. Most were clinging tightly to their mothers, some were snivelling, and one little boy was wailing loudly.

Sophie's mother glanced anxiously at her, but her daughter's only reaction was to pull down her dark eyebrows in a frown of disapproval.

"Fancy crying!" said Sophie.

"Let's hang up your anorak," said her mother. "There are some pegs in the corridor outside. Let's see if we can find yours."

If there was one word that Sophie was confident of reading it was her own name, and she had no trouble in spotting it. Beside each peg a child's name was printed on a picture of an animal – a lion, an elephant, a parrot, a rabbit. Sophie's picture was of a black-and-white cow with a big udder.

"Yikes!" said Sophie softly. "They knew!"

Sophie's mother felt that this might be a good moment to slip away. She kissed her, and said, a little tremulously, "See you later."

"Alligator," said Sophie in her usual no-nonsense way, and plodded back into the classroom.

It just so happened that the reception class teacher was also beginning her first term at the school, so that all the children, new and old alike, were strange to her.

Mostly they were strange to Sophie too, as she sat where she had been told to sit and stared stonily at the others. Suddenly her expression changed from one of suspicion to one of active dislike.

Sitting on the other side of the room was a pretty little girl with golden hair done in bunches that were tied with ribbon. This child, whose name was Dawn, Sophie had met once before and an unhappy meeting it had been.

Dawn had been invited round to Sophie's house to play, and had deliberately squashed one of Sophie's largest woodlice. In return, Sophie had taken Dawn's toy pony, a pink pony with a long silvery mane and tail, called Twinkletoes, and had jumped up and down on it until it was a dirty squashed lump whose toes would never twinkle again.

Now, unaware of Sophie's sultry glare, Dawn chattered brightly with her friends, until the teacher called for quiet. Then she told the new children that each of them would have an older child in the class to look after them until they knew their way around the school.

"I know my way round," said Sophie.

"Do you?" said the teacher. "How clever of you ... let me see, you are...?"

"Sophie."

"How clever of you, Sophie. I expect you have an older sister in one of the other classes?"

"No."

"An older brother then?"

"No."

Sophie loved guessing games.

"Go on," she said. "Try again."

"She's got *two* older brothers," piped up

Unaware of Sophie's sultry glare,
Dawn chattered brightly with her friends.

Dawn. "They're twins."

Sophie glowered furiously at her, but the teacher only said, "It's Dawn, isn't it? Yes, well, you seem to know all about Sophie's family, so you can look after her."

"Yuk!" said Sophie, folding her arms and sticking out her lower lip, while the smug smile on Dawn's pretty little face vanished abruptly.

When the bell rang for morning break, the teacher made sure that each new child had its escort before letting them go. Dawn, carrying a new blue pony, stood nervously before Sophie.

"D'you want to go to the toilet?" she said.

"No," said Sophie.

She did – like mad – but she had already determined that she would do nothing that Dawn suggested.

Out in the playground, the whole school ran screaming and yelling and skipping and jumping. The twins came to make sure (because they had been told to make sure) that Sophie was not unhappy.

They found her standing in a corner, glowering at the madding crowd. Nearby, but not too near, stood her minder, Dawn.

"You OK?" shouted Mark, and, "You all right?" yelled Matthew.

Sophie nodded. Her expression, which was funereal, did not change.

The twins looked at Dawn, who was anxiously clutching the blue pony.

"What do you want?" they said together.

"I'm s'posed to be looking after her," Dawn said.

"She your friend?" said Matthew to Sophie.

"No."

"D'you want her hanging round?" said Mark.

"No."

"Well, get lost!" they both shouted, and off Dawn ran.

Sophie began to jig from foot to foot.

Her brothers regarded her with practised eyes.

"D'you want to go?" asked Mark.

"Yes."

"D'you know where to go?" asked Matthew.

"Yes."

"Well, go then!" they both said, and off Sophie ran.

One of the Bad Things that had worried Sophie about Going to School had been Having to Eat School Lunches, especially pilchards in tomato sauce which she hated, and at lunch-time she plodded into the hall feeling sure that, today of all days, it would be pilchards. To her great delight, it was sausages and chips and baked beans, followed by apple crumble and custard, both favourites of hers; and not even having to sit next to Dawn stopped her from enjoying her lunch very much.

From then on everything seemed to improve, for in the afternoon they drew pictures to take home and show their parents.

Sophie loved drawing. She worked away with her coloured felt pens, dark head bent, tongue sticking out with the effort. All the other children in the class drew pictures of their mothers or fathers, or sometimes of their houses, but Sophie's was quite different from the rest.

"What a lot of things you're putting in

your picture, Sophie," said the teacher when she came round to have a look. "What is it meant to be?"

Sophie looked at her scornfully.

"Can't you see?" she said.

"Well, I wasn't quite sure…"

"I'll show you," said Sophie, and with a red felt pen she wrote across the top of the picture in big wobbly capitals:

MY FARM

"That's *very* good, Sophie," said the teacher. "Fancy you being able to write like that, and spell correctly too! You're a bright one! D'you think you'll be a writer when you grow up?"

"Of course not," said Sophie. "I'm going to be a lady farmer."

"What have you got there, Sophie?" said her mother when she came to collect her. Sophie was carrying her drawing rolled into a scroll, with an elastic band round it.

"I did a picture," she said.

"Can I see?"

"When we get home, Mummy," Sophie said. "It's a present, you see. For you. And Daddy. And Matthew and Mark, I suppose."

"What's it of?" asked the twins.

"My farm."

"Your toy farm?"

"No, my real one, that I'm going to buy with my Farm Money, when I'm a grown-up lady."

At home Sophie would not undo the scroll, but waited till her father had come home from work. Then the whole family gathered round the kitchen table for the

The whole family gathered round the kitchen table
for the Exhibition of Sophie's Picture.

Exhibition of Sophie's Picture, the result of her labours on her first day at school.

"That's very good, Sophie," said her father. " 'My Farm', eh?"

"No, mine," said Sophie.

"I was just reading out what you had written."

"It's beautiful," said her mother doubtfully.

But the twins were not prepared to leave it at that. They knew all about the animals that Sophie proposed to have, and they demanded to be shown the whereabouts in the picture of Blossom and April and May and Shorty and Measles the pig.

There seemed, however, to be a great many more animals in the picture than these – dozens in fact, though it was anybody's guess which of the squiggly little figures were cows and which hens or horses or pigs.

"What are those?" asked Matthew, pointing to a group in one corner.

"Pigs of course," said Sophie.

"They look more like sheep," said Mark.

"Sophie's an impressionist," said her father, "and it's a great picture. But you seem to have got an awful lot of animals on your farm, considering that you're planning to begin with just those five. How will you manage that?"

"I'll breed them of course," said Sophie. "Farm animals have lots of babies. I should have thought you'd have known that."

"Yes. How silly of me."

"What's this little black thing here?" asked her mother, pointing.

"That's Tom."

"Your cat?"

"Yes."

"And what's this brown thing over here?" said Mark. "Like a heap of something."

"It is a heap of something," said Sophie. "It's the dung-heap."

"Look," said Matthew. "There's a pair of legs sticking out of the top of it, as though someone had fallen in it head first."

"They have," said Sophie. "That's Dawn."

Dawn soon gave way to the disapproval
of the twins and the dislike of Sophie.

IN WHICH DUNCAN
COMES TO TEA

Dawn soon gave way to the disapproval of the twins and the dislike of Sophie. She sat by her charge or lined up beside her when she was told, but otherwise she steered well clear.

Sophie for her part was already looking forward to the time, some two years ahead, when she would be a Junior and could thus do Judo. She would throw Dawn down on the mat with a terrible crash.

When the term was a fortnight old, the headmistress was talking to the reception teacher about the new intake, asking how they were getting on.

"What about the twins' sister, Sophie?" she said.

"Small but very determined," was the reply.

"How does she get on with the other children?"

"She didn't seem to think much of any of them to start with. I paired her off with Dawn, but that doesn't seem to have been a good move."

"Bit of a loner, is she?"

"She does rather keep herself to herself."

Sophie's mother was also worried.

"I know you don't like Dawn," she said, "but what about the other girls in your class?"

"Don't like any of them."

"The boys then?"

"They're silly."

"All of them?"

"Duncan's all right."

Duncan, Sophie's mother found out later, was a very small boy, the smallest of all the children in Sophie's class. Sophie, she was told on asking the teacher, made use of him at playtime. Each held one end of a skipping-rope, and then Sophie would stand still while Duncan moved in a circle around her.

"I was on playground duty today, watching them," the teacher said, "and she says to him 'Walk on!' and 'Trot!' and 'Whoa!' just as though she was lunging a pony."

Shorty! thought Sophie's mother.

Indeed when Duncan was pointed out to her, she could see that he might well have Shetland blood in his veins. He had a shaggy mane of ginger hair, short legs and a fat stomach.

Not long after that, Sophie came home with another farmyard drawing. It was much the same as the original, including the little black figure of the cat Tom, but this time there were no legs sticking out of the dung-heap. Instead, there was a short matchstick figure standing beside it.

"Who's that?" her mother asked.

"That's my farm labourer. He's chucking the cow-muck on the heap."

"What's he called?"

"Duncan."

Sophie's new friend (or more properly, it seemed, her slave, since he instantly obeyed every order that she gave him) had of course been spotted by the twins.

"Sophie's got a boy-friend," said Matthew that evening.

"Called Duncan," said Mark.

"He is not my boy-friend," said Sophie. "I've told him he can come to work for me. On my farm. When we are grown-ups."

"And what did he say to that?" asked Sophie's father.

"He said he would, of course."

"Of course. But how will you afford to pay him?"

"I shan't."

"You mean he won't get any wages?" He'll have to work for nothing?"

"Not for nothing," Sophie said. "He'll get his food. I've told him he can have free milk from my cows and free eggs from my hens and free cornflakes from my corn."

"Lucky boy!"

"He is," said Sophie. "I've told him so."

At half-term, Duncan came to tea. Sophie had told him to ask his mummy if he could, so of course he did; and then the two mothers fixed it up between them, mindful of Sophie's instructions that he should bring his

"You have to be firm with earwigs," Sophie said.
"Don't stand any nonsense."

wellies and that there should be crumpets and chocolate Swiss roll.

Before tea, she took him down to the potting-shed to show him her flocks and herds. She was a little disappointed that he seemed nervous of them, especially the earwigs.

"They bite," Duncan said.

"Load of rubbish," Sophie said. "No good being scared of animals if you're going to be a farm labourer."

She picked one out of the shoe box labelled YEAR WIGS.

"You have to be firm with them," she said. "Don't stand any nonsense."

She pointed to the sack-covered seed tray.

"That's my cat's bed," she said. "He's called Tom. He's very big and black."

Duncan did not look too happy at this news.

"Where is he?" he said.

"Oh, somewhere about," said Sophie, airily.

She did not notice that Duncan shot anxious glances around him as they made their way up the darkening garden. But no one could fail to notice that he enjoyed his tea. As well as the crumpets and the chocolate Swiss roll, there were sandwiches and biscuits and a fruit cake, and the budding farm worker ploughed his way through the lot.

"He'll be sick," whispered Matthew.

"Or burst," whispered Mark.

"He's going to be ever so expensive for Sophie to feed," they said to one another.

Duncan was still eating when everyone else had finished, and might, it seemed, have gone on for ever had Sophie not told him to get down, they were going to play with her toy farm, he must do the milking.

Later, when Duncan's mother had come to collect him, they were standing at the front door, waving goodbye, when suddenly there was a terrible racket somewhere in the depths of the dark garden. It was a horrible yarring, yowling, whining, wailing chorus of dreadful voices, competing, it seemed, to see who could make the most awful noise.

"Yikes!" cried Sophie. "Whatever's that?"

"Cats, fighting," said her mother.

"It might be Tom!" Sophie said, and ran inside for a torch.

Though she would not have admitted it, Sophie felt a bit scared as she crossed the lawn, shining her torch about, for it was very dark and the caterwauling was very eerie.

Suddenly there was an explosion of spitting and snarling, and in the torchlight

*In the torchlight Sophie saw three dark shapes
rush across the grass.*

Sophie saw no less than three dark shapes rush across the grass, over the wall and away. All cats are grey at night, they say, but one of the shapes, Sophie was almost sure, looked really black.

"Tom!" she called. "Tom!" But the garden was silent now.

Not till Sophie had plodded back across the lawn and gone indoors did a distant voice answer.

"Yee-es?" it said enquiringly, but Sophie had shut the door.

*As soon as Sophie woke, she jumped out
of bed and went to her window.*

IN WHICH AUNT AL
HAS AN IDEA

"Why were those cats making all that row?"
Sophie asked later.

"Two toms, fighting, I expect," her father
said.

"There's only one Tom – my one."

"All male cats are called toms."

"Why were they fighting?"

"Over a female, I should say."

"I bet my Tom won."

"I've told you before," her mother said.
"He's not yours."

As soon as Sophie woke next morning, she
jumped out of bed and went to her window.
It was barely light, but she could see that

there was a black cat sitting in the middle of the lawn, looking up at her window with his orange eyes.

Sophie crept downstairs and opened the back door, stuffing her feet into wellies. She hurried round to the lawn but the cat had gone.

"Tom, Tom," she called, keeping her voice down so as not to wake the rest of the family, and to her joy a voice answered, "Yee-es?" or that's how it sounded to Sophie. Out of the shrubbery he came to be stroked, and then he followed her back into the kitchen.

"Have some milk, my dear," Sophie said, and filled a saucer, which Tom quickly emptied.

"Now listen, Tom," said Sophie. "You can't stay in the house, they'd only get angry, so I'll have to put you out again. But come back tomorrow morning and I'll give you some more milk, understand?"

"Yee-es," said the cat.

And indeed it seemed he did, for from now on he was waiting at the back door every morning.

"It's a funny thing," said Sophie's mother at breakfast one day, "but we seem to be using much more milk than usual. I keep having to ask the milkman for extra. Are you boys drinking more than you ordinarily do?"

"No," said the twins. "We don't much like the stuff, you know that, Mum."

"Sophie?"

Sophie stuck rigidly to the truth.

"I like milk," she said. "That's partly why I'm going to be a lady farmer. But I'm not drinking more than usual."

All might have been well, had not Sophie's father needed to go to Scotland on business.

73

"Sophie, get that animal out of here this minute!"

This meant catching an early train, and Tom was just enjoying his saucerful and Sophie was enjoying watching him, when her father came into the room.

"So that's where the extra milk is going!" he said. "Sophie, get that animal out of here this minute!"

"But Daddy…"

"No buts. Out!"

"Come, Tom," said Sophie with dignity. "Daddy doesn't like cats."

"I certainly don't like somebody else's cat drinking our milk," said her father. "Cats are only good for one thing and that's catching mice. That cat does not come into this house again, Sophie, d'you understand?"

"Never?" said Sophie.

She looked so woebegone that her father relented a little.

"I'll tell you what," he said, "if ever anyone sees a mouse in this house, then we'll think about having a cat."

"And don't think you can go putting saucers of milk out in the garden, Sophie," said her mother later, when she had heard all about it. "Cats should be given water to drink anyway, milk just makes them fat. And that cat's fat enough already." She should have known that Sophie, though small, was very determined, and if she had been about early enough in the days that followed, she would have seen that Sophie had no intention of giving Tom up. She did not let him in, and she did not give him milk, but she saw to it that there were scraps of some sort put out for his breakfast every morning.

Soon it was plain that Tom had forsaken his owners, whoever they were. Whether they were unworried by his disappearance, or whether they had moved house or gone to another district or abroad, no one ever knew, but the black cat had clearly adopted Sophie's garden as his territory and Sophie as his mistress. Now he even slept in the potting-shed.

Sophie was delighted of course. If only Daddy liked cats, she thought. If only we had mice in the house. But it was lovely to be continually meeting Tom in the garden, and lovely to be in bed at night and think of her black cat hunting in the black night outside.

"I bet Aunt Al will like you," she said to Tom. "Daddy's bringing her back with him, for a visit, when he comes home from Scotland. She lives in the Highlands, you know. They have Wild Cats there. Would you like to meet a Wild Cat?"

"Nee-o," said Tom.

When Aunt Al did arrive, apparently as fresh as a daisy after so long a journey, Sophie lost no time.

"Come and see Tom, Aunt Al," she said.

Aunt Al, small and birdlike with a sharp beaky nose, looked at Sophie with her head on one side.

"Who's Tom?" she said. "Your boy-friend?"

"No, that's Duncan," said Matthew.

"Tom's a cat," said Mark.

Aunt Al turned to her great-nephew.

"I thought you didn't like cats," she said.

"I don't," said Sophie's father. "And it is not allowed in the house."

"It's a stray," said Sophie's mother. "It seems to have adopted us. I've rung the police and the RSPCA but no one has claimed it."

*Aunt Al, small and birdlike, looked at
Sophie with her head on one side.*

"They have," said Sophie. "I have. It's my cat."

Tom seemed to take to Aunt Al straightaway. He came out of the shrubbery and wrapped himself around her thin bird's legs and made his steam-engine noise. Aunt Al scratched the roots of his ears.

"So you can't come indoors?" she said.

"Nee-o," said Tom.

"Only if we have a mouse in the house, Daddy says," said Sophie.

"Which is highly unlikely, I suppose," said Aunt Al.

The very next day was one of those lovely mild early spring days full of promise, and in the afternoon Aunt Al and Sophie were walking round the garden together. Sophie was carrying the yellow bucket in which she collected fresh creatures for her flocks and herds, to replace those who had decided to leave.

They came to the potting-shed, and there inside was Tom, crouching low.

"He's caught something," Aunt Al said, and sure enough there was a mouse between his forepaws, perhaps the same fat mouse that Sophie had found eating Christmas cake. It was alive and, though bedraggled, apparently unharmed, but every time it tried to crawl away, Tom raked it back.

"Poor mouse!" Sophie cried. "Leave it, Tom!" But the black cat only growled at her.

"Cats eat mice, you know," said Aunt Al. "It's quite natural. He won't let you take it away from him."

"He will!" said Sophie. "I'll make him!" and she moved towards him in a most determined manner, swinging her yellow bucket threateningly.

With a cry that sounded remarkably like "Yikes!" Tom shot out of the shed.

"We can't just leave it here," said Sophie, looking at the mouse, so shocked that it was too afraid to move. "Tom will come back. What shall we do, Aunt Al?"

"Hang on half a tick," said Aunt Al. "Got an empty box somewhere? I've just had a brilliant idea."

Thus it was that, later on, Sophie and her mother and her great-great-aunt were having tea in the kitchen, when Aunt Al suddenly said, "What was that?"

"What was what?" said Sophie's mother.

"I thought I heard a little scratching noise. As though there was a mouse somewhere in the room."

With a cry that sounded remarkably like "Yikes!" Tom shot out of the shed.

"There are no mice in this house," said Sophie's mother. "I can tell you that for sure."

"I'm certain I heard it," said Aunt Al. "Listen, there it is again!"

"It's over in that corner," Sophie said. "Somewhere by that old cardboard box."

Sophie's mother got up from the table and went over to the box and lifted the lid. Then she shut it again quickly.

"Oh!" she cried. "It is a mouse! Oh, I don't like mice! Sophie, take it out into the garden."

When Sophie had done as she was told, she plodded back into the kitchen.

"Mummy," she said. "I told you what Daddy said, didn't I?"

"What?"

"'If ever anyone sees a mouse in this house,' he said, 'we'll think about having a cat.' So when Daddy comes back from work we can tell him we've seen a mouse, can't we?" Sophie's mother looked at them both, the five year old and the eighty-one year old. Their faces were expressionless.

Hers broke into a big smile.

"You wicked pair!" she said.

It was plain to everyone that, now and for ever, he was Sophie's Tom.

IN WHICH DAWN
TAKES A TUMBLE

Tom proved himself to be a very tactful animal. He was careful not to take advantage of his new position as a house cat. He did not mew to be let in or out, he did not claw at curtains, or jump on chair covers with dirty feet, or worse. He did not make a nuisance of himself in any way.

He steered well clear of Sophie's father as though aware of his distaste for cats, and he kept away from the twins, suspecting that they might tease him. He was polite to Sophie's mother, but it was plain to everyone that, now and for ever, he was Sophie's Tom.

Sophie, on the other hand, was not a tactful person. Not content with being allowed to have Tom indoors, she demanded that he sleep on her bed.

"No," her mother said firmly. "Don't push your luck, Sophie. Daddy's being very good about all this, he's even having a cat-flap put in the back door; and I'm buying the tinned meat for Tom, and that's quite enough to be going on with."

Sophie, however, got her way in an unexpected fashion.

About a week after Aunt Al's visit, Sophie came home from school saying that her head itched.

"Whereabouts?" her mother asked.

"Everywhere in my hair," said Sophie, scratching away in her dark mop.

"Head lice, I expect," said Matthew.

"Or fleas from the cat," said Mark, and they beat a hasty retreat.

Later, when Sophie was in the bath, her mother noticed that there were spots on her back, dark, pink, flat spots, and she called the doctor.

"Keep her in bed for a while," the doctor said. "She's got a bit of a temperature. It's chicken-pox."

"I haven't been near any chickens," Sophie said.

The doctor laughed.

"Try to stop her scratching the spots," he said to Sophie's mother. "Anything you can think of to distract her? What does she specially like doing?"

"Drawing," said her mother.

"And playing with my cat," said Sophie.

"Good," said the doctor. "Well, you stay in bed for a couple of days, and have your cat with you, and then you can draw her."

"Him," said Sophie. "Bring Tom, please, Mummy."

"Only in the daytime," Sophie's mother said when the doctor had gone. "This cat goes outside at night."

But that didn't last long either. Sophie always left her bedroom door open, and Tom came in through the cat-flap as and when he pleased and sneaked upstairs like a shadow. And a rather fat shadow too – he was getting positively tubby. Sophie woke each morning to feel the warm weight of him on her feet.

Apart from sitting for his portrait dozens of times, Tom proved a blessing during Sophie's chicken-pox, for, whenever she felt she *must* scratch her spots they itched so much, she scratched Tom instead, and that of course he much enjoyed.

Meanwhile, at school, several other children in Sophie's class had caught chicken-pox, though not, Sophie would have been sorry to hear, Dawn.

Dawn, moreover, was not slow to take advantage of Sophie's absence. She had not forgotten or forgiven the squashing of Twinkletoes, and now she quite deliberately set out to ensnare Sophie's future farm labourer. It was not difficult, for Duncan was not only a biddable little boy but very greedy. Regular offers of sweets from Dawn quickly made him her slave, and he followed her about with the same dog-like devotion he had once shown to Sophie.

Dawn should have known better. Setting herself up against Sophie was rather like a toy poodle challenging a bulldog, and she lived to regret it.

At morning break on her first day back at

school, Sophie went out into the playground carrying her skipping-rope. Part of the game she had invented, with herself as horse-breaker, was to go out into the paddock (the playground) and call the pony (Duncan). Then, when he came obediently trotting up, she would attach the lunge (the skipping-rope) to his harness (hand), and the training would begin.

Now she plodded out again into the noisy throng of children and called "Duncan! Duncan! Come up, come up, good boy!"

She had trained him to whinny in reply to this summons, but now she heard no answer. Then she saw, at the far end of the playground, a sight to make her blood boil. It was Dawn, lunging Duncan! In her left hand she held the blue toy pony, in her right the end of a skipping-rope, while Duncan marched solemnly around her.

Sophie plodded across the playground and stood, just outside Duncan's circle, and glowered at Dawn.

"What are you doing with my pony?" she said.

Dawn waved the blue toy.

"It's not yours," she said, "it's mine, and don't you touch it or I'll tell Miss."

"I don't mean that pony," said Sophie.

Duncan, meantime, having last received the command, "Walk on!", walked on, and since Dawn was not turning with him, for she feared to take her eyes off Sophie, he walked in ever-decreasing circles, till at last the rope was wrapped tightly round Dawn's legs and Duncan was brought to a halt. Dawn was cocooned, like a big fly parcelled up by a little spider.

Sophie stumped up to the two prisoners.

"You," she said to Dawn, "are mowldy,

*"And as for you," Sophie said
to Duncan, "you're sacked!"*

stupid and assive," and she gave her a push in the chest so that they both fell down.

Sophie listened with pleasure to their howls, and then addressed her would-be farm labourer.

"And as for you," she said, "you're sacked!"

"You should have seen it, Mum!" said the twins, when their mother came to collect the three children after school.

"Dawn was bawling her head off!" said Mark.

"And Duncan was bawling his head off!" said Matthew.

"And the teacher on duty came up ..."

"And said, 'Whatever's going on?' ..."

"And Dawn said, 'She pushed me' ..."

"And the teacher said, 'Who pushed you?' ..."

"And Dawn said, 'Sophie'..."

"And the teacher said, 'Did you, Sophie?'..."

"And Sophie said, 'Yes'..."

"And the teacher said, 'Why?'..."

"And Sophie wouldn't answer."

"So what happened then?" asked their mother.

"Sophie had to go to the headmistress," said Matthew.

"In her office," said Mark.

"And what did the headmistress say?"

"We don't know," they said. "We listened at the keyhole, but we couldn't hear."

"What did she say, Sophie?" asked her mother.

"She said I was naughty."

"And what did you say?"

"Nothing."

"So what did she do?"

"Made me stay in all of the next play-time," said Sophie.

She grinned.

"I drew a picture," she said.

She took a piece of paper out of her satchel. It was one of her standard farmyard scenes, but this time there were two pairs of legs, one long and skinny, one short and fat, sticking out of the top of the dung-heap.

*The twins' eighth birthday fell in late April, and
Sophie was busy thinking what to get them.*

IN WHICH SOPHIE
GETS A SURPRISE

The twins' eighth birthday fell in late April, and Sophie was busy thinking what to get them.

"It's difficult, you see," she said to Tom, "to know whether to buy them the same things, which is a bit boring, or different things, when one might like his present more than the other."

She stroked his fat black stomach.

"What do you think?" she said, but he only purred.

She sought her father's opinion.

"I should ask them what they want," he said. So she did.

"What would you like for your birthday,

Matthew?" she said to her elder brother.

"A radio-controlled model car," he said.

"And I want one too," said Mark.

"Oh," said Sophie. "What kind?"

"A Lamborghini," said Matthew.

"A Dune Buggy," said Mark.

"Oh," said Sophie.

"How much do they cost?" she said.

"About £50," they said.

"£50 the two?"

"No, £50 each."

"Oh," said Sophie.

She took her Farm Money out of her piggy-bank. There was Aunt Al's £5 note and quite a lot of coins that she had saved. She sought her mother's help in counting them.

"You've got 47p there," her mother said. "So that's £5.47p altogether."

"I don't think I can afford the sort of things the twins want," she said to Tom later.

"Nee-o."

"I suppose I could cut the £5 note in half."

"Nee-o."

Sophie rather agreed with him. She was not mean by nature, but that would have been over generous.

"You're right, Tom. It'll have to be the 47p. And it'll have to be sweets as usual. They like sweets."

So next time they went shopping, she told her mother that she was going to spend 47p buying sweets for the twins' birthday present.

In the shop, almost the first things to catch Sophie's eye were chocolate pennies.

"How much are those, Mummy?" she said.

Her mother looked.

"A penny each."

"So I could buy forty-seven of them?"

"Yes."

So she did.

Afterwards she said, "Mummy, what's half 47p?"

"Let's see … it's 23½ p. Only there aren't halfpennies any more. If you wanted to split it, it would have to be 24p and 23p."

"Oh blow," said Sophie. "That's no good. They must have exactly the same number of chocolate pennies."

"Take one away," said her mother. "Then there'll be twenty-three for Matthew and twenty-three for Mark."

"Take one away? But what shall I do with it?"

"Open your mouth and shut your eyes, and I'll give you something to make you wise."

*"Open your mouth and shut your eyes,
and I'll give you something to make you wise."*

After carefully dividing the chocolate pennies into two heaps (she could count to twenty-three now), Sophie had then put each heap into a little cardboard box, had written the twins' names on each box, and then put LOVE FROM SOPHIE on both. The boxes were part of a store that she kept in the potting-shed, but Matthew and Mark were not aware that they had once been used for keeping black beetles in.

When the day came, they were delighted with Sophie's presents.

"Gosh, thanks, Sophie!" they said.

"That's all right."

"Must have cost you an awful lot," they said.

"It did. 47p."

By chance the birthday was on a Sunday, which meant that the children's father was at home, and what's more, it was a beautiful sunny spring day. Matthew and Mark had each been allowed to ask three friends to tea, so they chose six boys with whom they regularly played football.

"Would you like to ask someone, Sophie?" her mother said.

"Darling Dawn?" said Mark.

"Or dearest Duncan?" said Matthew.

"Yuk!" said Sophie. "No thanks. I'll just have my friend Tom."

"You give that cat too much food," her father said. "He's as fat as butter. He needs to take more exercise. Which reminds me – boys, do you want to have the Olympic Games again?"

"Oh yes, please, Dad!" they cried.

The previous year their father, who was keen on that sort of thing, had organized all sorts of running and jumping and throwing competitions, and they had called them "the Olympic Games". There were races, short ones across the lawn and long ones right round the garden, and high jump and long jump, and throwing the discus (a tin plate) and tossing the caber (a clothes prop) and putting the shot (a brick).

So this year they did the same, and one or other of the twins, who were good at that sort of thing, won nearly everything, or else dead-heated for first place.

Sophie went in for every event and was always last because she was much the smallest, but everyone cheered her for her determination. And in the last race of all, the marathon, everyone had to run six times round the garden while Sophie was allowed to run only three times, and she won!

Then they all ate an enormous tea.

After all the guests had gone, Sophie plodded upstairs to play with her farm before bedtime. It had grown quite a bit since Christmas, for Sophie had either bought or been given a number of new animals, including a goat and some geese and a good few more cows. So big was it now that she had been allowed the use of the attic room at the top of the house so that the farm could be permanently laid out there on the floor. In the attic were some old bits of furniture and various oddments, and there was even an off-cut of carpet, grassy-green in colour, on which the animals stood or lay or grazed.

Sophie knelt on the floor, the black cat purring at her side. With one hand she stroked him, with the other she began to

"Time for milking," Sophie said.
"Time for bed," said her father.

move the dairy herd.

"Time for milking," she said.

"Time for bed," said her father's voice.

He came in and sat down in a broken armchair.

"Come on, my old farmer," he said. "You must be tired, specially after winning a marathon."

"In a minute, Daddy, I've got to get the cows in first."

She began to use both hands to pick them up, and Tom, released, jumped on to her father's lap. To her amazement, he was not only allowed to remain there, but she saw her father was actually stroking him!

"Daddy!" she said. "I thought you didn't like cats!"

"I don't," he said. "Except this one. I've got used to him, I suppose. You're a good boy, Tom, aren't you?"

"Nee-o," said the black cat.

"Oh yes, you are. Come on, Sophie love. Beddy-byes."

As soon as she woke the next morning Sophie felt that something was different. What? Oh yes, there was no black hot-water bottle on her feet. She got dressed and went out to see to her flocks and herds. There was no sign of Tom in the potting-shed, or anywhere in the garden, and stranger still, he did not appear at breakfast-time, which was when Sophie usually fed him.

By the time she had finished eating, Sophie was becoming rather worried, though she did not say anything to the others. She plodded upstairs to the attic to do the morning milking.

As she neared the door, she suddenly heard some faint little squeaks. They seemed to be coming from the old armchair. Sophie went to look in it, and then she gave a cry of "Yikes!"

In the chair, snuggling against the now much smaller stomach of Tom, were four little furry bodies. One was tabby, one was tortoiseshell, one was black with a white bib and white feet, and the fourth was coal-black, just like its mother.

"Oh Tom!" Sophie said. "How clever you are, my dear! And all this time I thought you were a boy. Whatever am I going to call you now?"

But the only answer was a loud proud purr of contentment from Sophie's Tom.

THE

END